Little Life Lesson books

I Have Diabetes

A Children's Book about Juvenile Diabetes

Written and Illustrated
By Karri Andersen

This Book is dedicated to our

Kindra

You are our blessing and inspiration.

My name is Kindra.
I would like to tell
you about my
Diabetes and me.

I got very sick and I was not getting better . I felt so tired and frustrated. I didn't even want to play.

Then I got very thirsty
and was drinking a lot.

I also had to go to the bathroom a lot.

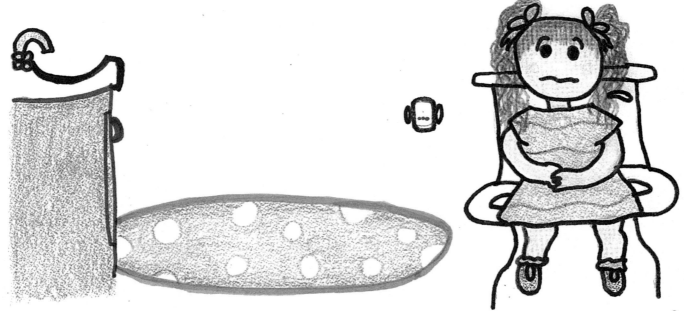

I went to the doctors.
They poked my finger to
check my blood. The doctor
said, "You have Diabetes".
"What is Diabetes?" I asked.

The doctor told me that Diabetes is when my body needs help to digest the food and sugar I eat. The medicine that I need is called Insulin. It gives the food and sugar I eat to the rest of my body and keeps me healthy and strong. Otherwise the sugars stay in my blood and I feel sick.

We were glad to find out why I was sick so I could get better.

We went to stay at the hospital. There were Doctors and Nurses there. They like to help the kids get well and not be sick. I was so brave.

I had a lot of shots
and finger pokes. I even had an IV that
stayed in my arm. It hurt a little and
sometimes I was sad. My family was sad too.
They love me so much and they wish I
didn't have to get poked. But it is very
important that they take good care of me. 7

My Family learned how to give me my
shots and check my blood. I never knew
my blood had numbers. I thought that
was pretty neat! We check my blood
all the time. Now it barely even hurts.

I can have shots or a pump to get my insulin into my body.

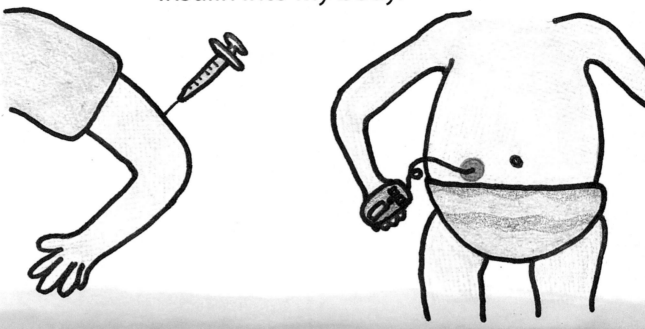

I have a blood monitor that tells me my blood sugar numbers.

One day I will do my shots and test my blood all by myself!

I always need to check with a grownup before I eat or drink anything. Sometimes they say "not now" and that is fine with me. That is how I help take care of myself.

All my friends like to watch me have my blood checked and get my shots. They think I am so tough.

I always tell a grownup if I feel like my blood sugar is Low or High.
Sometimes I feel ....

Very Angry or Mad,

Thirsty or Hungry,

Sweaty or Hot.....

Sleepy
or Tired,

Sad or
Frustrated,

SHAKY OR WEAK,

Or I just don't feel right.
It is always good to check your blood
and make sure your blood numbers are ok. 14

Now I am used to my Diabetes. It doesn't even bother me anymore. I have met a lot of kids who have Diabetes too and we are just like all the other kids.

The End….

Note to Parents and Family of a Diabetic Child,

I hope you and your loved ones find comfort in this book. I remember those tough days when we were first diagnosed. I know that this can be a trying time in our lives when we find out that we (the caretakers and children) have a life altering decease called diabetes. It has been my experience that your child will react to this situation the same way you do. Even though it is very hard and frustrating at first it does become easier. Try to see the bright side of things. Focus on the great new medications and medical devices that we have. Educate yourself on the earlier days of type 1 diabetes and how far we have come to improve our quality of life. This will also give you hope for the future and finding a cure. Be more aware of your diet and focus on how you and your family are all going to take better care of your health. The biggest thing is the fact that your child is so brave! Always make every blood test and injection a proud moment for you. Explain how important it is that they take care of themselves. Remind them all the time you are doing this because you love them!

You are not alone. There are many organizations and support groups around and I urge you to find some and get involved. Some of the best support and education I have gotten is from other families. Your child will also find comfort in being around other kids in the same situation.

I wish for every diabetic child to feel like they are just like all the other kids and to know that their bodies just work a little different. For them to know they are not alone, to be strong, to have a great support system and stay healthy. Good luck to everyone who is enduring this new life adventure... Sincerely,

Karri Andersen

$14.95 12/20/17

LONGWOOD PUBLIC LIBRARY
800 Middle Country Road
Middle Island, NY 11953
(631) 924-6400
longwoodlibrary.org

LIBRARY HOURS

Monday-Friday	9:30 a.m. - 9:00 p.m.
Saturday	9:30 a.m. - 5:00 p.m.
Sunday (Sept-June)	1:00 p.m. - 5:00 p.m.